The Cock, the Mouse, and the Little Red Hen

For Mari

First U.S. edition 1992
First published in Great Britain in 1991 by Walker Books Ltd., London.

ISBN 1-56402-008-8

Library of Congress Catalog Card Number 91-71857
Library of Congress Cataloging-in-Publication information is available.

10 9 8 7 6 5 4 3 2 1

Printed and bound in Hong Kong by
South China Printing Co. (1988) Ltd.

Candlewick Press
2067 Massachusetts Avenue
Cambridge, Massachusetts 02140

The Cock, the Mouse,

and the Little Red Hen

A Traditional Tale

ILLUSTRATED BY GRAHAM PERCY

CANDLEWICK PRESS
CAMBRIDGE, MASSACHUSETTS

Once upon a time there was a hill, and on the hill was a pretty little house. It had one green door and four windows with green shutters. And in this house lived a cock, a mouse, and a little red hen.

On a hill nearby, there was another little house. It had a door that wouldn't close and two broken windows and no paint at all on the shutters. And in this house lived a bold bad fox and four bad little foxes.

One morning the four bad little foxes were complaining to the big bad fox.

"We had nothing to eat yesterday," said the first little fox.

"And scarcely anything the day before," said the second.

"And only half a chicken the day before that," said
the third.

"And only two little ducks the day before that," said
the fourth.

So the big bad fox got his sack and said he would go to the pretty little house on the other hill and catch the cock, the mouse, and the little red hen for dinner.

"I'll light a fire to roast the cock," said the first little fox.
"I'll put on a saucepan to boil the hen," said the second.
"I'll grease the frying pan to fry the mouse," said the third.
"And I'll have the biggest helping when they're cooked,"
said the fourth, who was the greediest of all.

Meanwhile, at the pretty little house, the cock and the mouse had woken up cross and quarrelsome. But the little red hen was bustling about, looking as bright as a sunbeam.

"Who'll get some sticks to light the fire?" she asked.
"I won't," said the cock crossly.
"I won't," said the lazy mouse.
"Then I'll do it myself," said the little red hen.
  And she bustled out to get the sticks.

"Now, who'll fill the kettle from the spring?" asked the little red hen.

"I won't," said the cock.
"I won't," said the mouse.
"Then I'll do it myself," said the little red hen.
And she bustled out to fill the kettle.

"Who'll get the breakfast?" asked the little red hen
when she had put the kettle on to boil.

"I won't," said the cock.
"I won't," said the mouse.
"Then I'll do it myself," said the little red hen.
   And she laid everything on the table.

All during breakfast, the cock and the mouse quarreled and grumbled. The cock made the tablecloth dirty, and the mouse dropped crumbs on the floor.

"Who'll help clear up?" asked the little red hen when they had eaten.

"I won't," said the cock.

"I won't," said the mouse.

"Then I'll do it myself," said the little red hen.

And she cleared everything away and swept the hearth.

"And now, who'll help me make the beds?" she asked.

"I won't," said the cock.

"I won't," said the mouse.

"Then I'll do it myself," said the little red hen.
  And she bustled away upstairs.

The lazy cock and mouse sat in their chairs and dozed by the fire. They didn't see the big bad fox peering in at the window.

RAT-A-TAT-TAT! The fox knocked at the door.
"Who can that be?" said the mouse, opening one eye.
"Go and see for yourself," said the cock rudely.
But the mouse, not bothering to see who
was outside, lifted the latch and
opened the door.

In leapt the big bad fox!

"Oh, oh, oh!" squeaked the mouse, running for the chimney.

"Cock-a-doodle-doo!" screamed the cock, jumping up from his chair.

But the fox was too quick for them. He scooped up the
mouse and the cock and put them both into his sack.

And when the little red hen came running downstairs to
see what all the noise was about, the fox caught her too.

He tied a length of string around the neck of the sack,
threw it over his shoulder, and set off down the hill.

"Oh, oh, oh!" cried the cock as they bumped along.
"I'm sorry I was so cross."
"Oh, oh, oh!" wailed the mouse. "I'm sorry I was so lazy."
"It's never too late to change," said the little red hen.
"And look—I still have my work basket. I'll soon be busy."

Now the fox began to think that the sack was rather
heavy, and at last he stopped to rest.

The moment the little red hen heard him snoring, she
took out her scissors and snipped a small hole in the sack.

"Quick," she whispered to the mouse. "Run and fetch a
stone just as big as yourself."

The mouse ran out and came back in no time at all, rolling a stone before him.

"Push it into the sack," said the little red hen.

Then she snipped at the hole until it was a bit bigger.

"Quick," she said to the cock. "Run and fetch a stone just as big as yourself."

The cock flew out and came back in no time at all, rolling
a stone before him. This, too, was pushed into the sack.
Then the little red hen popped out. She fetched a stone
just as big as herself and pushed it in with the others.

Next, the little red hen took her needle and thread from her work basket. In a twinkling she had sewn up the hole in the sack.

When it was done, the cock, the mouse, and the little red
hen ran home as fast as they could.

When the big bad fox woke up, the sun had sunk low in the sky. He hoisted the sack over his shoulder and staggered on down the hill.

At the bottom of the hill was a stream, which he had to cross. Splish! In went one foot. Splash! In went the other. SPLOSH! The sack was so heavy that the fox tumbled into a deep pool.

Then the fish carried him off, and he was never seen again. And the four greedy little foxes had to go to bed without any supper.

The cock, the mouse, and the little red hen were quite out of breath when they got home. They bolted the door, closed the shutters, and pulled down the blinds.

"Now," said the little red hen, "who will stoke up the fire and put on the kettle?"
"I will," said the cock cheerfully.
"I will," said the mouse with a twirl of his whiskers.

So, when the tea was made,
the little red hen drew up her chair
and sat contentedly by the fire.